P9-DBS-821

BEACH LANE BOOKS

An imprint of Simon & Schuster Children's Publishing Division

1230 Avenue of the Americas, New York, New York 10020

Copyright ∘ 2014 by Petra Mathers

BEACH LANE BOOKS is a trademark of Simon & Schuster, Inc.

For information about special discounts for bulk purchases, please contact Simon & Schuster Special Sales

at 1-866-506-1949 or business@simonandschuster.com.

The Simon & Schuster Speakers Bureau can bring authors to your live event.

For more information or to book an event, contact the Simon & Schuster Speakers Bureau

at 1-866-248-3049 or visit our website at www.simonspeakers.com.

Book design by Ann Bobco

The text for this book is set in Deepdene.

The illustrations for this book are rendered in watercolor.

Manufactured in China

0714 SCP

First Edition

2 4 6 8 10 9 7 5 3 1

Library of Congress Cataloging-in-Publication Data

Mathers, Petra, author, illustrator.

When Aunt Mattie got her wings / by Petra Mathers.—First edition.

p. cm.

Summary: When Aunt Mattie dies, best friends Lottie and Herbie console each other and celebrate Aunt Mattie's life by scattering her ashes
and preparing her favorite snack—peanut butter and jelly sandwiches (with bananas).

ISBN 978-1-4814-1044-1 (hardcover)

ISBN 978-1-4814-1045-8 (eBook)

[1. Death—Fiction. 2. Grief—Fiction. 3. Friendship—Fiction. 4. Chickens—Fiction. 5. Ducks—Fiction.] I. Title.

PZ7.M42475Wh 2014

[E]—dc23

2013037476

When Aunt Mattie got her wings

by petra mathers

BEACH LANE BOOKS

New York   London   Toronto   Sydney   New Delhi

"Herbie," said Lottie, "City Hospital just called. Aunt Mattie's getting very weak.
 I'm leaving on the early bus."
"I'll take you to the station," said Herbie.
 I can always count on my best friend, Herbie, Lottie thought.

"How come Aunt Mattie's sick, Lottie? She's
 a nurse."
"She isn't sick; she's ninety-nine years old."
"Wow," said Herbie.

"You mean it's like her motor is all worn out?"
"That's right, Herbie. I don't know when I'll
 be back."
"I'll miss you, Lottie."

Lottie watched the familiar landmarks whiz by.
How often she had made this trip to visit her
aunt. Hopewell Tunnel was coming up next.

"Hopeless Terror" Herbie called it, since they
got stuck there once in a traffic jam.

How often they had picked up Aunt Mattie, always with her nursing bag, ever ready for any emergency.

In all those years they must have motored hundreds of miles back and forth to Pudding Rock . . .

. . . and eaten thousands of peanut butter
and jelly sandwiches.
"OPEN WIDE," Aunt Mattie would say to
the cooler.

On her last visit, Herbie had fixed a trivet
to Aunt Mattie's cane so it wouldn't sink
into the sand.

When Lottie arrived at City Hospital, the head nurse rushed up to her. "Your aunt's in Room Twenty-Four. She says she likes looking at the billboard across from there. Now she's mostly sleeping, wants no food or drink. She asked for you."

Aunt Mattie looked tiny in the big hospital
bed. Her breath was heavy and whistled a little.
"Aunt Mattie," said Lottie.

There was no answer.
This may be the last time I'll spend with my aunt,
thought Lottie.

Hours passed. Lottie felt chilly and leaned against the radiator. It was getting dark but someone was still playing badminton on the lawn.

"Aunt Mattie, remember that day in the park?"

"The guy who swallowed the birdie?   'OPEN WIDE,' you said."

Aunt Mattie opened her eyes.
"Lottie, you're here. We don't have much
  time. Will you help me with my cap?

"They are expecting me upstairs, but I told
  them I was waiting for you. Oh, Lottie,
  what fun we've had.

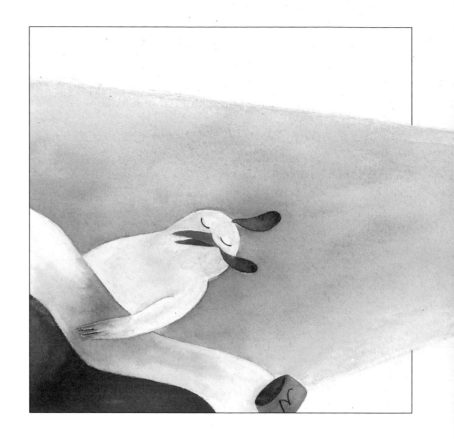

"They are calling again. They know I'm
 ready now."
"Auntie," was all Lottie could get out.

"I can see them at the gate. We are ready for
 takeoff. Farewell, dearest Lottie, farewell."

Meanwhile, Herbie had arrived.
"Hopeless Terror, my eye! Just wait till Lottie
sees me."

He froze at the door. Was Lottie crying?
He had never seen her cry before.

"Lottie, I drove through the tunnel all by myself!"

"Herbie, you came! Aunt Mattie just died. I am so sad."
"I'm here now, Lottie. We are together."

When the team from the funeral home picked up Aunt Mattie, City Hospital came to a standstill to watch the passage of its most beloved nurse.

Lottie and Herbie went to stay at Aunt
Mattie's apartment.
"Why was Aunt Mattie smiling, Lottie?"
"I think she was happy, Herbie . . .

". . . she said someone was meeting her at
the gate."
"The gate of heaven?"
"It sounded more like an airport, Herbie."

Upstairs a letter was waiting for them.

Dear Lottie and Herbie,
By the time you read this I will be dead, and I imagine you're feeling a little down in the beak. That's why I'm writing this letter. I've had a long and happy life doing what I loved best: being a nurse and spending time with you. Sometimes I dreamed of getting on a plane to see the world, but then I thought of you and got on the bus to Oysterville instead. Now it's time to make room for someone else on this earth. I have arranged to be cremated so you can take my ashes home with you and scatter them between Oysterville and Pudding Rock. There I'll always be near you, mixed in with sand and sea.

Lots of love always,
Your Aunt Mattie

P.S. Globe for Lottie, cookie jar for Herbie, all else for Nurse's Vacation Fund.

"I miss Aunt Mattie. It hurts right here."
"Me too. It's heartache, Herbie. Come sit
by me. I am so glad you are here."

"Doesn't it feel like Aunt Mattie should be here?"
"She is, Herbie, in our hearts."
"Maybe our hearts ache because Aunt Mattie
is moving into them."

After three days they could pick up the urn
with Aunt Mattie's ashes.

There wasn't much talk on the way home.
Each was thinking their own thoughts.
"The sky is crying," Herbie finally said.

"I'm glad we'll be there soon," said Lottie.
"It's easier to be sad at home."

After settling in, Lottie took a look at Aunt
Mattie's globe. Little pins stuck everywhere,
all her dreams of Faraway.

On the first fine day Herbie called early.
"Today's Aunt Mattie's Day."
"I'm almost ready, Herbie. Meet you at the bottom."

"Ahoy, Lottie, hop aboard."
"Aye, aye, Captain."
"Where is Aunt Mattie?" asked Herbie.
"In the cooler," said Lottie.

"What else is in there?"
"Aunt Mattie's special with bananas."
 Near Pudding Rock, Herbie cut the engine.

They took their time scattering the ashes,
taking turns and watching them float away.

"Lottie," said Herbie, "if you could go anywhere in the world, even to where Aunt Mattie is now, where would you go?"
"I'd go have a picnic at Pudding Rock with my best friend, Herbie," said Lottie.

And so they did.